THE LITTLEST LEAGUER

D0038539

Story and pictures by

SYD HOFF

SCHOLASTIC INC.
New York Toronto London Auckland Sydney

No part of this publication may be reproduced in whole or in part, or stored in a retrieval system, or transmitted in any form or by any means, electronic, mechanical, photocopying, recording, or otherwise, without written permission of the publisher. For information regarding permission, write to E.P. Dutton Inc., 2 Park Ave., New York, NY 10016.

ISBN: 0-590-05385-X

Text and Illustrations copyright © 1976 by Syd Hoff. All rights reserved.
This edition is published by Scholastic Inc., 730 Broadway, New York, NY 10003, by arrangement with E.P. Dutton.

19 18 17 16 5 6 7/9

Printed in the U.S.A. 40

THE LITTLEST LEAGUER

BUS
TO
BALL
FIELD

Of all the players in
the little league,
Harold was the littlest.

"Maybe you ought to go home
and come back next year,"
said Shirley the shortstop.

"Maybe you ought to go home
and not come back at all,"
said Big Leon, who played
first base because he had
such a long reach.

This only made Harold try harder. He tried in the infield, but ground balls did not have to take much of a hop to go over his head.

He tried in the outfield,
but the other outfielders had
longer legs and could move
under a fly ball faster.

Harold tried to make up for all this as a hitter, but there seemed to be no bat light enough for him and balls zoomed past him before he could swing.

"Please don't feel badly,
but I'm afraid there's only
one place I can put you,"
said Mr. Lombardo the coach.

He put Harold on the bench. Harold sat there, game after game, wearing out the seat of his pants.

Sometimes he took care of
the team's bats.

Sometimes he brought them
cold drinks.

"I'm tired of being so little,"
thought Harold, and he stayed
out in the rain when a game
was stopped hoping it would
make him grow like the flowers.

All it did was make him wet.

"Maybe you ought to try eating green vegetables," said Shirley when the team went home.

"Better still, try forgetting where we play," said Big Leon.

That night Mr. Lombardo came to Harold's house. He knew his littlest leaguer needed cheering up.

"You're letting your size bother you. There have been many great baseball players who were not tall," said the coach. And Harold's father agreed with him.

The two men talked about short players who were in the Baseball Hall of Fame, and Harold listened until he had to go to sleep.

So Harold kept sitting on the bench, game after game, until it was the last game of the season. The winner of this game would be the Little League Champions. The score was nothing to nothing.

Harold watched Shirley
catching line drives and making
great plays at shortstop.
But in the top of the third
the score was still nothing
to nothing.

He watched Big Leon using his long reach to take throws from all over the infield and get runners out at first base. But in the top of the seventh the score was still nothing to nothing.

"Oh, if I could only help them, *really* help them," thought Harold, as his team came in to take their final turn at bat in the last half of the ninth inning.

"Move over," said Big Leon,
shoving him off the bench.

Harold sat on the ground knowing he didn't deserve to sit with the team. He just kept sitting there, thinking of all those short players in the Baseball Hall of Fame.

Then with two out, the next three batters got infield hits and Harold's team had the bases loaded.

"Ow-www!" cried a voice.

It was Big Leon getting ready
to bat. He had stepped in
a hole and twisted his foot.

"I can't walk on it, I can't even stand on it," said Big Leon as they helped him back to the bench.

"Harold, it's up to you now.
We need a hit to win. The bases
are loaded and all our pinch
hitters are sick from
too many cold drinks. Will you
please go to bat for us?"
asked Mr. Lombardo.

Harold walked to the plate.
He stood as tall as possible,
hoping to scare the pitcher.

But Knuckles Smith,
the opposing pitcher,

threw a fast ball
right across the plate.

"Strike one!"
shouted the umpire.

Knuckles wound up and
pitched again.
This time he threw his curve.

"Strike two!"
shouted the umpire.

On the bench, Harold's team groaned. Some of them got ready to leave. "It's all over," said Big Leon.

Then Harold got an idea.
He crouched at the plate as
small as possible. He crouched
so low, and became so small,
that Knuckles could not find
the strike zone.

The next pitch came towards
the plate, but it was too high.
"Ball one!" shouted the umpire.

Knuckles threw again and again, but one pitch was too low and the other was too wide. The count was three balls and two strikes.

The next pitch would decide everything.

"Come on, Harold!" shouted Shirley on the bench.

"Keep your eye on the ball!" shouted Big Leon.

"Make him put it where you want it!" shouted the rest of the team, and Mr. Lombardo looked as if he was praying.

The ball floated towards the plate. It was Knuckles Smith's slow ball, his change of pace, which always fooled batters.

Harold closed his eyes and
swung with all his might,
and — POW! — he connected!

The ball was going, going, gone over the fence for a home run. Harold ran around the bases, from first to second, from second to third.

He crossed home plate and
his team mates picked him up
and carried him on their
shoulders.

"Harold, you may be the littlest leaguer, but today you were the biggest leaguer of them all," said Mr. Lombardo. And even Big Leon was cheering.